My Best Friend Is Moving

by David Parker
Illustrated by Margeaux Lucas

Scholastic Inc.
New York Toronto London Auckland Sydney
Mexico City New Delhi Hong Kong Buenos Aires

To my college roommate.
— D.P.

To my beloved friend Kim Patton-Bragg.
— M.L.

ISBN-13: 978-0-545-00389-6
ISBN-10: 0-545-00389-X

12 11 10 9 8 7 6 5 4 3 2 1   7 8 9 10 11 12/0

Printed in the U.S.A.
First printing, October 2007

Chapter One
My Best Friend

Kathy is my best friend.
We see each other every day.
"Let's play catch," says Kathy.
"Great! Then we can go on the
swings," I say.

Later we take a walk.
Then we sing a song we made up.
"Listen to the joke that my cousin told me," I say.
"You always tell the funniest jokes," she says.

We like the same things…especially ice cream.
Kathy says, "Pumpkin is my favorite flavor."
"Mine, too," I say.

We like to watch movies together.
Our favorite movie is about a dog
named Pepper.
"I always cry when the dog gets lost,"
I say.
"Me, too," Kathy sniffles.

Sometimes we play make-believe.
"That hat looks great on you," I say.
"I'm going to wear the yellow
boa today."
"We're ready for the camera,"
giggles Kathy.

We like to help others.
"Thank you for carrying these bags
inside for me," says Mrs. Williams.
"Call us any time," I say.
"It feels good to help," says Kathy.

We are in the same class at school.
"Did you finish your reading
homework?" she asks.
"I did the math first," I say.
Kathy and I help each other solve
our problems.

We do everything together.

Even our parents are friends.
Our moms laugh together at the
playground.
Our dads fire up the grill for summer
picnics.

Chapter Two
That's Not Fair

My parents sit me down after school.
They look serious.
"I talked with Kathy's mom today," says
my mother. "They are moving."

"That's not fair!" I shout.
"We know this is upsetting for you,"
says Mom.
"It's okay to be sad," says Dad.

"How can they do that to us?" I cry.
I am too sad to talk.
I am too mad to listen.
My best friend is moving.

I have a lot of questions.
"Where are they moving?"
"When will they leave?"
"Who will I play with?"
I am very confused.

"Who will sit next to me at school?"
"Why do they have to move?"
"How can we see each other?"
"Those are all good questions,"
says Mom.
"Let's try to answer them together,"
says Dad.

"Things will be different, but Kathy will still be your friend," says Mom.
"We share so many things!" I shout.
"Can you think of some ways you can still share?" asks Dad.
I do not want to, but I will try.

Chapter Three
A Different Kind of Friendship

"I heard that you are moving,"
I tell Kathy.
"I don't want to go," Kathy says.

"There are a lot of ways that we can still be friends," I say.
"That's true. We can always talk on the phone," she replies.
"And we can send e-mails after school," I say.
"We can write letters like we do when we're on vacation," she says.

"My brother says we can use a
camera to see each other on the
computer," she adds.
"My sister says she will help me make
videos for you," I say.

"I'll send you pictures of fun things I've done," I say.
"I'll record songs that we make up and send them to you," she says.
"And we can watch TV on the phone together sometimes," I say.

"Maybe we can visit each other,"
I say.
"Our families can go away together,"
says Kathy.
"We'll still share a lot of things, Kathy,"
I say.

Moving day isn't much fun.
"I'm going to miss you," says Kathy.
"I'll miss you, too," I say.
We give each other a big hug.
Then Kathy gets into her parents' car
and drives away.

"How are you feeling?" Mom asks.
"I'm sad, but I know Kathy and I will stay friends," I say. "I've already written her a letter."
"If you send it now, it'll be waiting at her new house when she gets there," says Dad.

"It doesn't matter where Kathy lives,"
I say. "She'll still be my best friend."

What would *you* do if your best friend
moved away?
How would *you* keep your friendship
strong?